To Erin,
With Love,
Organik &

♡ Harlie Girl

Waf!

This book belongs to:

_____

To my daughter Ava, the joy of my life
and to Charlie Girl, our favorite poodle and best friend.

And in honor of all the dogs in the world
who make us happy every day.

PENNY BLACK PUBLISHING

New York, New York

First Edition Printing 2013

Copyright 2012 Charlie Girl LLC.
ISBN: 978-0-692-01929-0

LIBRARY OF CONGRESS No. 0000TXU0018091750201

Printed in the United States by Bookmasters, Inc.
30 Amberwood Parkway, Ashland, OH 44805
February 2013 Job# M10427

Inset cover photograph by Jill Wachter.

Charlie Girl

"Tails" of a Very Original Poodle

Written & Art Directed by Elizabeth Frogel
Illustrations by Ashley Quigg

PENNY BLACK PUBLISHING
New York, New York

Charlie Girl

"Tails" of a Very Original Poodle

Hi. I'm Charlie Girl.
I'm 2 ½ years old.   That's a teenager in dog years!

I live a very busy life in the glamorous City of New York.
Even though I have my very own fancy bed,
I prefer the more comfy sofa.

Did I mention that I almost live in a tree house?
Well, really, I live up above the trees
in a fabulous apartment building
overlooking Central Park.
I see green for miles on end!

My Mother is a fashion designer. I don't know what my Daddy does, but every morning I bring him his Wall Street Journal to read with his breakfast, and he tells me whether he's going to buy more Kibble today; or wait 'til tomorrow.

I'm just glad Mom feeds me Kibble when I'm hungry!

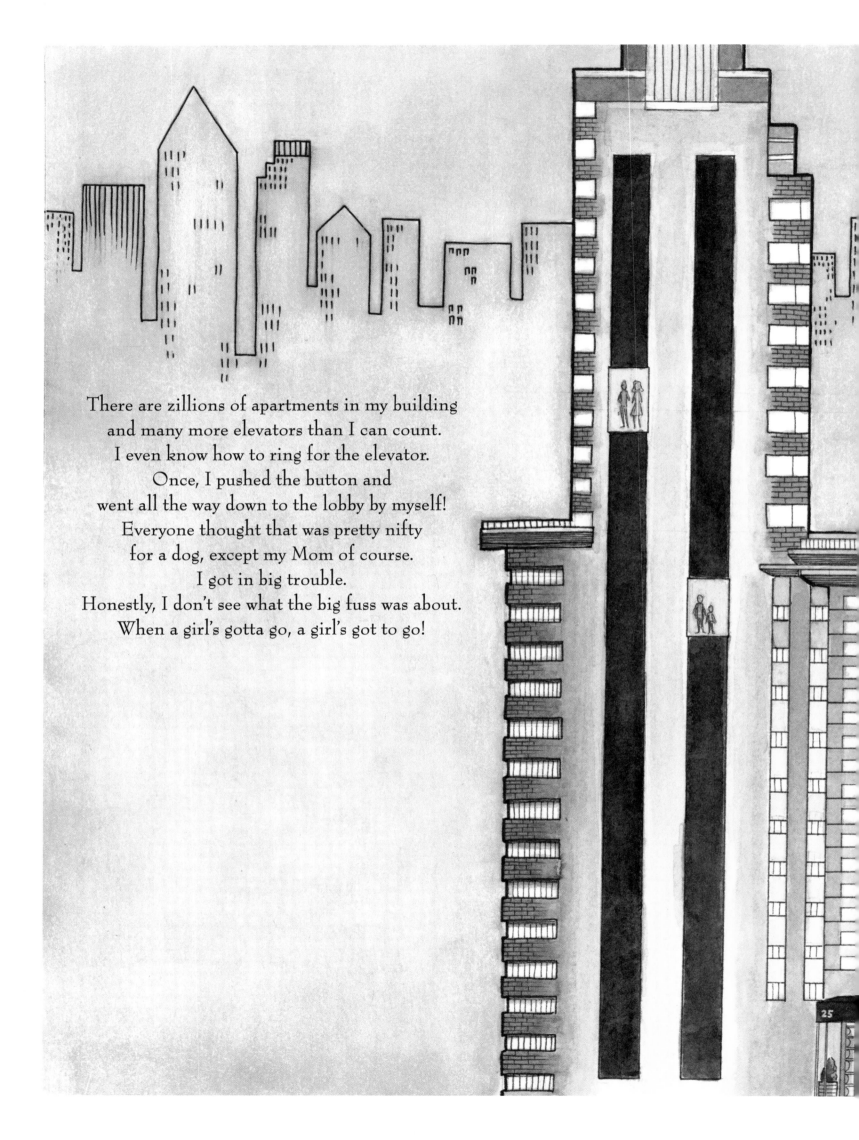

There are zillions of apartments in my building
and many more elevators than I can count.
I even know how to ring for the elevator.
Once, I pushed the button and
went all the way down to the lobby by myself!
Everyone thought that was pretty nifty
for a dog, except my Mom of course.
I got in big trouble.
Honestly, I don't see what the big fuss was about.
When a girl's gotta go, a girl's got to go!

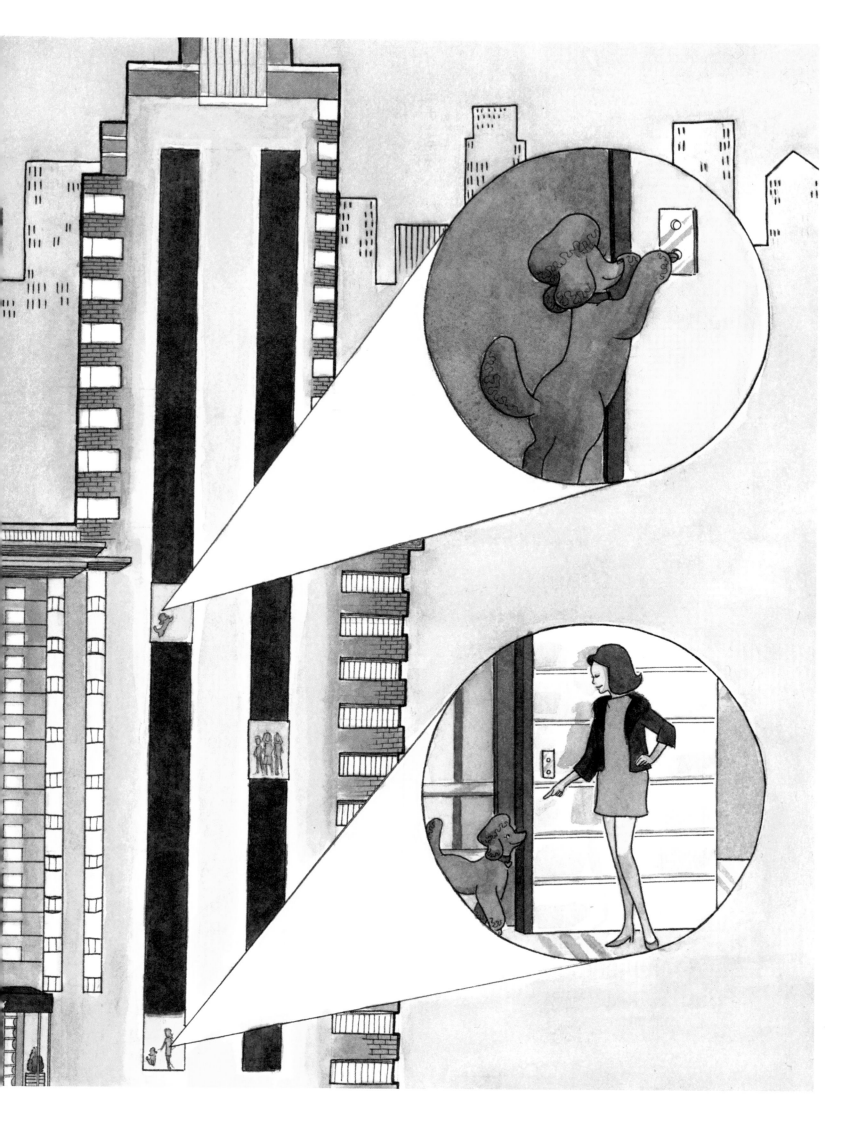

There are lots of people who work in our building; doormen, elevator men, and
Tommy who runs the package room. I know everyone and everyone knows me.
My favorite is William the doorman because he was there when I came home as a pup.

Then, there's Hugo. Sometimes, he let's me wear his hat and pretend I'm a doorman.
I once asked Hugo why there aren't any doorgirls. "Gee Charlie, I really don't know.
Maybe you'll be the first doorgirl when you grow up." "I certainly will!"

And how could I forget Jose; he always has a joke ready and waiting.
Sometimes Mom says he should have his own TV show.

And to me apartment living is the way to go. Holidays in my building are celebrated to the hilt, especially Halloween! Every Halloween all the children and dogs get dressed up in fancy costumes and we have a big parade in our lobby.

My first Halloween I went as a blushing bride! Last year I dressed up as Elvis. Most of the kids didn't know who Elvis was…but I told them, he was a big rock star in the 60's and 70's. My Dad tells me he was the king. But he never told me of what country. The only king I know of is the king of England.

Every morning I get to run in the big patch of green outside my window. It's Central Park. I meet my friends in the same spot every morning. I get so excited I drag my mother behind me as we zigzag down the path into the park.

My best friend is Sky. She's a Collie like Lassie, only prettier.
She was my first friend and we go way back! She taught me how to wrestle and chew on each other's ears. Sky always has a lot to say and the only time her mouth is closed is when she has a treat in it.

Sky has a strange attraction to anything with wheels, especially bicycles and roller blades. She chases after any wheels she sees. Her mother goes crazy when she does this and all we can hear in the park is her yelling, "Skyyyyy, nooooooo!" But that doesn't stop Sky!

On the other hand, my addiction is with pastries. I can always smell when there's a bagel, a muffin, or a doughnut nearby. The nose always knows! My hunting skills sure do come in handy sometimes.

I have lots of other friends too and what a cast of characters we are. Lizzy the Labradoodle is a mix between a Poodle and a Labrador. Then there's Tucker and Jackson, the Wheaton Terriers.

There's also my friend Tootsie, like the candy. She's a pint size version of me!

Don Wrinkles the Pug. His face is smooshed in like he ran into a wall, but we don't tell him. Maggie the German Shepherd, Floof the Briard and Cinnamon the Golden Retriever.

I take Cinnamon's favorite ball every day and she chases me around yapping
"give it back Charlie Girl!"

I may look like a very glamorous girl, with my stylish hairdo, but don't be fooled, I'm a very sporty girl! I can jump high in the air and catch my Frisbee, and when I do, my friends all cheer, "Way to go Charlie Girl!" And when it's time to go, Mom lures me over with a fabulous treat.
It works every time.

Then I go home and collapse for a very long nap. But before I'm allowed through the front door, Mom says, "Let me see those paws, Miss Charlie Girl. Charlie how do you always get so dirty?" "I don't know Mom, just playing in the park I guess."

By the way, did you know that Standard Poodles are actually retrieving dogs? I didn't know that either. I guess that makes sense because I do love to fetch over and over. But I've got to admit those hunters get up way too early for me, at the crack of dawn I hear. Personally, I like to sleep in.

Sometimes on really sunny days in New York, my family and I head to the boathouse in Central Park to rent a boat. I get really excited to get close to the ducks and swans, but Dad just can't row fast enough sometimes. "Faster Dad, faster, I've got some ducks and swans to scare." When I get really close I go "boo!" and I giggle to myself as they go flying away. And Mom calls after, "Charlie Girl that's not nice." But it's still funny to me.

I really love my walks. Our neighbors are so nice.
Whenever I leave the building, I hear
"Charlie Girl, how are you today?" Or sometimes,
"Charlie Girl, I love your new haircut!"
And my favorite thing to hear is,
"Hey Charlie, you're such a cutie!"
I love being popular, but I try *not* to brag.

After a nice walk, Mom tells me the plan for the day.   She's already dressed, and now it's my turn to get ready.   She always says, "Great accessories make the woman."

I have many different collars and leashes that I wear depending on my mood or sometimes, to match my mother's spiffy outfit. When the weather gets rough, I get to wear my snappy plaid raincoat. But at the end of the day, a girl can never go wrong with a simple string of pearls.

And, in New York, dogs are welcome just about everywhere! I love riding in the car and especially taxis. I love hanging my head out the window and feeling the wind rush through my hair. Mom pulls me back in and says, "Charlie Girl, don't hang your head and paws out the window. Please sit tight! We'll be there soon." It's when the taxi finally stops, I know the real fun is about to begin. We're going shopping!

My Mom and I love shopping. My Dad says Mom and I could win gold medals if it
ever becomes an Olympic sport.

One of our favorite places to go shopping is the make-up counter at Bergdorf Goodman. Carmen always helps me with cream for my paws and picks out great new colors for my Mom. We do a lot of walking here in New York and Carmen says, "One has to take good care of one's paws."

In fact, Mom and I walk almost everywhere. We meet many new and exciting people during our excursions. Sometimes we see famous celebrities along the way and they actually want to meet me! Poor Mom, they always want to talk to me first. But she's still first to me! Shopping builds up our appetites and Mom will remind me that we need to grab some lunch before we finish the rest of our errands. I can hardly wait!

We especially like the outdoor cafés along Madison Avenue. "Hurry up Charlie Girl!" Mom says. "We've got to get to our favorite table before somebody gets it first." I love to meet my friends there and my Mom knows just the perfect table.

While Mom and her friends chat, my pals and I wait for the table scraps to fall right into our mouths! After my belly is full, sometimes we like to hit the galleries...

New York is a very cultural city. There are lots of art museums and galleries.
The other day we were invited to an art gallery downtown.
The featured artist was Andy Woofhal and Mom told me I'd like his work.
My favorite painting was the one of a giant Alpo can.
It was simple, but spoke my language.

Ahhhh, what a masterpiece!

A New York City dog always has to look her best. When I'm due for a haircut I get groomed at my favorite spa by a lady named Ella. Ella bathes me, cuts my hair, and even does my nails! She takes such good care of me. I always feel very special and prance out the door with new ribbons in my hair and lots of people complimenting me as we make our way home.

Mom and I have loads of fun all day. But another favorite part of my day is nighttime. Every night I wait patiently at the front door for my Dad to come home. As soon as I hear the front door open, I jump up to greet him and I give him a big kiss. He says, "Hey Charlie Girl, how was your day?" "Great Dad" I bark, "and I'll tell you all about it on our evening walk."

On the way back home, we stop to get the mail, which I personally deliver to my Mom.

Finally, at the end of a long day I get to jump in their bed and cuddle.   Suddenly I'm fast asleep,
dreaming about all of the wonderful things that may await me tomorrow...

More to come...

As Charlie Girl gets a sister,

experiences new adventures

and travels the world!